THE BEAST
OF
MONSIEUR RACINE

BY TOMI UNGERER

DEDICATION : *to Maurice Sendak*

Monsieur Racine was a retired tax collector who lived peacefully in a secluded cottage. He was content to spend his days shuffling about, watching birds and clouds, and tinkering with his little garden.

In this garden grew a pear tree that was Monsieur Racine's great pride. It bore fruit of extraordinary flavour and juiciness.

Pears from that tree had won him many prizes at local country fairs. Millionaires had offered great sums of money for his harvest.

"What do I want with all that money?" he thought. "The pears are mine, I love them, I eat them." There was no selling, there was no sharing. Monsieur Racine was a happy man.

But one morning, alas! three times, alas! he found all his pears gone.

Upon closer investigation, he discovered strange footprints the
predator had left behind. Footprints of a weird nature, indeed.
It looked as if the ground had been trampled by stumps rather
than feet.

"Outrageous, positively outrageous!" exclaimed the victim.
"Only a young elephant could have left such tracks."

One pear was still dangling from a high branch. "Ah-ha! One pear
left!" said Monsieur Racine. "I am sure the marauder will come
back for it. And I shall be here to give out the proper punishment."

He fetched some yarn and tied one end to the golden pear,
and the other to the bell hanging at the cottage entrance. Then
he put on his old cavalry uniform and squeezed himself into
its shiny cuirass. Facing the open door, he waited all day, his sabre
at the ready.

Hours passed by and Monsieur Racine fell asleep.

It was dusk when suddenly the bell started to jingle. Our avenger jumped to his feet and grabbed his sabre. "Sapristi!"

There in the twilight stood a beast, the strangest thing Monsieur Racine had ever set eyes upon.

It was large, about the size of a young calf.

From a distance it looked like a heap of mouldy blankets. Long, sock-like ears were flopping on both sides of a seemingly eyeless head. A shaggy, mangled mane topped a drooping snout. Its feet were like stumps, and it had baggy knees. It made no sound.

Monsieur Racine's anger gave way to curiosity. "It looks inoffensive enough," he muttered to himself as he came out of the cottage. The beast didn't budge and even seemed willing to strike up an acquaintance. So Monsieur Racine pulled a macaroon out of his pocket and, mounting it on the tip of his blade, presented it to the thing.

The friendly offering was acknowledged.

"More delicacies of this sort and it could be tamed," reflected Monsieur Racine. He went to his kitchen and fetched a wedge of apple tart, salami, pâté, and a bottle of red wine.

Man and beast picnicked heartily under the pear tree.

It was late and dark when the animal got up to depart. "Good night, gentle thing," said Monsieur Racine as he kissed his visitor on both jowls. "Come back tomorrow and we shall have a lovely time together."

Late every afternoon the beast came back, and every night it vanished into the forest it had come from.

It was especially fond of cookies, chocolate, and ice-cream. So eager was Monsieur Racine to please his guest that he installed, at great expense, a refrigeration system, to preserve vats of ice-cream delivered from the city.

On rainy days, they would just be cosy on the old sofa Monsieur Racine had inherited from his Aunt Sophie. Both friends enjoyed music. They listened religiously.

"I lost my pears but found a companion," thought the old tax collector.

On sunny days, when road conditions would allow it, he would
load the beast in a trailer pulled by his motricycle. Off they zoomed
with dizzying speed.

The animal was playful and Monsieur Racine built a whole playground for its rompings.

Some sight it was when the old man and his pet frolicked all over the place.

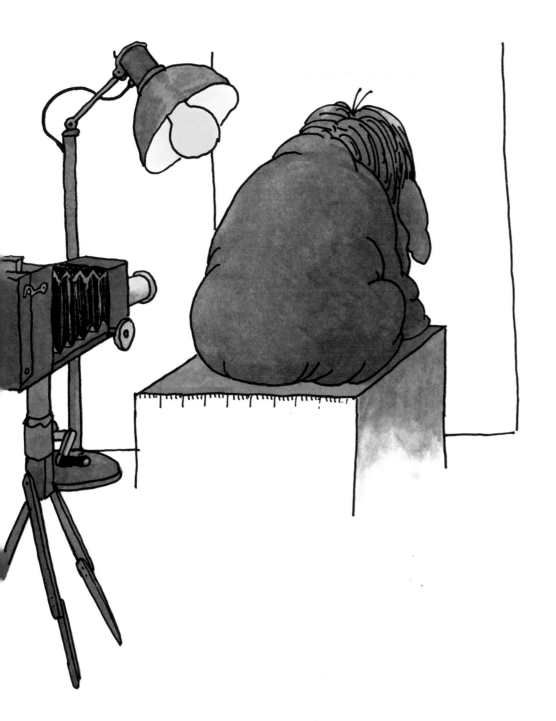

All the while, Monsieur Racine was studying the creature, taking photographs, making sketches, recording measurements. He found it unrelated to any other living form. Bodily tissues were lifeless, and the bone structure was non-existent. The whole body seemed to consist of a conglomerate of living lumps.

Monsieur Racine searched his library for a hint. Nothing.
The beast was unheard of.

So Monsieur Racine decided to write to the Academy of Sciences in Paris. With his letter he enclosed a meticulous study of the animal's living habits, as well as a set of photographs.

The answer was prompt. Monsieur Racine's discovery had created a sensation among the members of the Academy, and he was invited to Paris to present his find.

He went to work at once. With the help of his creature, he built a comfortable cage.

It was carted at government expense to the nearest railway station.

Their arrival in Paris was a triumph. The Mayor himself insisted
on welcoming the new French wonder.

Military bands escorted our friends to their hotel.
Reporters and photographers were everywhere.

Fortunes were offered for Monsieur Racine's animal by circus owners, zoo managers, and wealthy maniacs. "What do I want with money?" was his answer. "The beast is my friend, and friends are not for sale. And let that be that!"

The next day was the day.

The members of the Academy met in the amphitheatre. At ten o'clock Greenwich time, the door to the platform opened and Monsieur Racine walked in, fittingly dressed in a dark suit and followed by the beast.

There were "Ohs" and "Ahs" from the audience and unanimous applause. Some ladies swooned.

On the platform Monsieur Racine was now ready to make his presentation. "Messieurs, Mesdames, honoured members of the Academy…"

THEN something incredible happened.

The beast, which had always remained silent, broke into hysterical giggles. Shaking, rolling on its side, it ripped and tore itself apart.

Out of a pile of skins and rags emerged two children. The assembly was struck dumb and numb, then burst into an uproar. The police had to be called in to clear the amphitheatre.

When news of the hoax reached the crowds waiting outside, a riot began. Buses were overturned.

Unspeakable acts were performed.

What a mess! People are still talking about it.

But Monsieur Racine, who had a sense of humour, found the joke quite unique. After congratulating the children for their cleverness and endurance, he took them on a tour of the capital.

Then they went home and the children were returned to their parents, nice country folk who lived on the other side of the forest.

Monsieur Racine soon had a new crop of pears, which he happily shared with his two young friends.

Phaidon Press Limited
Regent's Wharf
All Saints Street
London, N1 9PA

Phaidon Press Inc.
65 Bleecker Street
New York, NY 10012

www.phaidon.com

This edition © 2014 Phaidon Press Limited
First published in German as *Das Biest des
Monsieur Racine* © 1972 Diogenes Verlag
AG Zürich

ISBN 978 0 7148 6081 7

007-0714

A CIP catalogue record for this book is
available from the British Library.

Printed in China